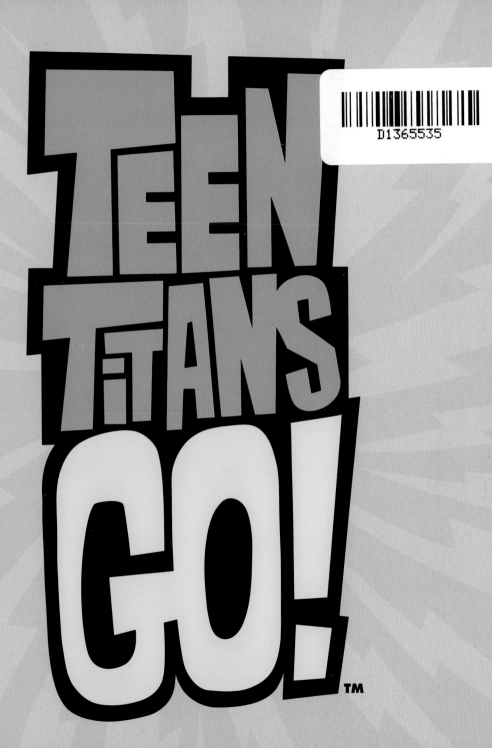

Cover design by Elaine Lopez-Levine.

Little, Brown and Company
Hachette Book Group
1290 Avenue of the Americas, New York, NY 10104
Visit us at LBYR.com

First Edition: October 2018

Little, Brown and Company is a division of Hachette Book Group, Inc.
Little, Brown and Company name and logo are trademarks of Hachette Book Group, Inc.

The publisher is not responsible for websites (or their content)
that are not owned by the publisher.

Library of Congress Control Number 2018935805

ISBNs: 978-0-316-51886-4 (pbk.), 978-0-316-51884-0 (ebook),
978-0-316-51889-5 (ebook), 978-0-316-51890-1 (ebook)

Printed in China

APS

10 9 8 7 6 5 4 3 2 1

BOOTY SCOOTY

Adapted by **Donald Lemke**
Based on the episode "Booty Scooty"
written by **Ben Gruber**

L **B**

LITTLE, BROWN AND COMPANY
New York Boston

Inside Titans Tower, Cyborg, Raven, Starfire, and Beast Boy are chilling on the living room couch. Suddenly…

"Guys! Guys!" a frantic voice shouts.

"Yo, it's Robin," says Beast Boy, spotting his teammate outside the Tower's gate.

"Let me in!" says Robin, gasping for breath.

"First, do the Booty Scooty," Cyborg says with a sly smile.

"Come on!" Robin groans. "Do I have to?!"

"Well, you ain't coming in till you feel the shame of that Boot-iss Scoot-iss, son!" adds Beast Boy with delight.

"*Ugh!* Fine!" he finally agrees.

Cyborg presses a button on his robotic chest. *Click!* A hard-hitting beat starts to bump and thump, and then...

"BOOTY!"

NOW DO THE BOOTY SCOOTY

Robin sadly shakes his heroic hind end to the thoroughly catchy tune.

"*Scoot, scoot, scoot that booty-booty!*" his teammates chant.

"*Scoot, scoot, scoot that booty-booty!*"

When the music finally stops, Cyborg, Starfire, Raven, and Beast Boy all laugh.

"You've been sufficiently shamed," Cyborg decides.

"Come on! I have news. Just open the latch!" Robin pleads. Starfire suggests a simpler idea. "The machine of Golden Rubes will handle that menial task for us."

To unlatch the gate, Cyborg places an anvil on a nearby conveyor belt. The anvil falls onto an air pump, which blows up a balloon until...

POP!

The balloon surprises a turkey...

...who lays an egg...

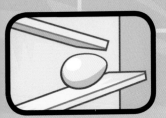

...that drops onto a mousetrap that slaps a monkey...

...who spits a banana at a lamp...

...that shines on a bat...

...which signals Batman...

...who tosses a football at a target and...misses.

"These things never work in real life!" Robin cries, then simply leaps over the gate.

"Huge news, guys!" Robin gasps. "Some rich land barons are planning on tearing down the Titans Tower and turning it into a shopping mall! We have to stop them!" yells Robin.

"But how?" asks Starfire. "The rich land barons have all of the monies."

"There's only one way to fight money," Robin boldly declares. "With more money!" He charges into Titans Tower. "Follow me!"

MOMENTS LATER...

"What is the object of our attic search?" Starfire asks.

Robin pulls out a dusty old treasure map. "This!"

Cyborg examines it. "A rare historical artifact like this has gotta be worth a fortune."

"In fact, this whole attic is filled with valuables," adds Raven.

"We could sell 'em for cash money and save the Tower, yo!" suggests Beast Boy.

"We're not selling the map or any of these other valuables," Robin says. "We are going on a super-dangerous adventure to find the treasure!"

The teammates follow the map deep beneath Titans Tower. Just then, a ghoulish cry echoes through the tunnels.

"What was that?!" Cyborg shouts.

"Oh, that's just the freak I keep chained up down here," Robin says. He leads the Teen Titans into a chamber, where an angry creature is chained to the floor.

"Oh man, he's nasty!" says Cyborg.

"He truly is the monster," Starfire agrees. "Guys, I think it just needs a friend," Beast Boy suggests, approaching the freak.

The creature sniffs Beast Boy like a hungry dog. "Veh-gee-tuh-buhls…" The freak drools.

"Oh! You want the turnip I keep in my pocket?" asks Beast Boy.

"More!" the freak demands. But Beast Boy is totally out of pocket veggie stock, so… *"RARRGHHH!"*

The Teen Titans flee from the creature, quickly ducking into another tunnel.

"I think we lost him!" Robin huffs.

Then Cyborg spots a strange instrument nearby. "Oh man, is that piano made of bones?" he asks. "*Super* nasty!"

"I've seen this before," says Robin. "We need to play the piano to open that door. But one wrong note and..."

SCHING!

"The pressure is intense, I know," Robin continues, "but one of you must volunteer—"

"I'll do it!" Cyborg, Raven, Starfire, and Beast Boy shout together. They are all expert piano players...obviously.

"Aw, yeah, let me get some!" Beast Boy pushes his teammates aside and busts out a rockin'—but totally wrong—tune.

"Beast Boy!" Robin yells for him to stop.

"Uh, my bad," says Beast Boy, returning to the correct notes.

Once he does, the door quickly opens.

"That's wassup!" Beast Boy grins.

The Titans continue through the booby-trapped tunnels until...
"A ladder!" Starfire observes. "But where does it lead?"
"To the living room," Robin answers knowingly.

"Wait!" Raven appears more annoyed than usual. "So we could have just climbed down the ladder and skipped the freak and the deadly piano thing?"

"Yeah," Robin confirms, "but where's the adventure in that?"

"I don't want no adventure," Beast Boy cries. "I wants my couch!"

"Don't you see? You may live *up there*, but down here you might *die*!" Robin exclaims. "Up there is a comfy couch and a TV. But down here, there is a freak! Down here, there is a bone piano and other horrors!" Robin clutches his fist heroically. "So who's with me?!"

Raven rolls her eyes. "Yeah, no thanks. We're going back."
Robin pulls out his flaming bo staff and immediately burns down the ladder.
"*Now* who's with me?" he asks.

Before the Titans can answer, the freak returns! *"RAHHHH!"*

The teammates sprint across a narrow, rocky bridge, when...

CRACK!

The bridge breaks, and the Titans fall down, down, down onto a perfectly placed waterslide, which spits them out into a giant underground cavern.

The cavern is filled with crazy-old pirate ships and...

"A giant octopus!" Starfire screams.

"If we want that treasure, we have to fight it!" Robin declares.

"Really? We're kinda running short on time. I feel like we should cut around this guy," Raven suggests.

"Fine." Robin sighs. "We'll skip the octopus."

"Apologies, my eight-legged friend," Starfire tells the saddened beast, and then kisses the octopus on its slimy forehead.

MOMENTS LATER...

"There it is!" cries Robin, spotting the treasure chest in the arms of pirate skeleton. Robin opens the chest, and the teammates gasp at all the riches inside.

"Peep those diamonds, yo!" Beast Boy exclaims.

"Forget the diamonds," says Cyborg. "Look at those ducats!"

"Doubloons!" Starfire coos.

"We rich!" Beast Boy declares.

"Yeah, we are," says Cyborg. "Now, let's get out of here."

The others agree. But before they leave, Robin drops one teeny-tiny jewel in the pirate skeleton's bony hand.

"This is for you, dead guy," Robin says gratefully.

"BLARGH!" The pirate's ghost suddenly appears from its skeleton.
"One gem?!" the ghost cries. "You steal my treasure hoard, and all
you leave to me is one measly gem?"

"In all fairness, we thought you were dead," Raven explains.

"I was!" the ghost shouts. "Dead and happy. Look, I am fine with someone taking my treasure, but did you have to insult me by giving me *this*?! One single gem!"

The angry ghost pulls a sword from his belt. *"NOW GIVE ME BACK MY TREASURE!"*

FWISH! The ghost slices a rope above Robin's head.

With that, a boulder falls from the ceiling onto a catapult...

...which launches a nasty skull onto a series of ramps...
...that lead down, down, down until...

PLOP!

The skull lands on the forehead of the lonely octopus...
...who tosses the skull at a nearby target and...misses.

"ACK!" the ghost-pirate-skeleton cries in disgust. "These things never work in real life!"

Frustrated, he simply presses the target himself, rocketing the Titans out of the cavern.

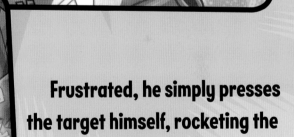

BACK ON THE LIVING ROOM COUCH...

"I can't believe it. We didn't get the treasure," Robin mopes. "It was right there. I guess I should have been more generous with that dead guy."

"I'm sure gonna miss this place," Cyborg says.

"A shame we will lose it to those despicable land barons," Starfire agrees.

When Freak has been sufficiently shamed, Beast Boy
wraps his arms around his new friend.
"I love you, Freak!" Beast Boy declares.
Freak smiles with delight. "That's what's up!"

Freak shakes his wretched rump to the hard-hitting beat.

"*Scoot, scoot, scoot that booty-booty!*" his friends cheer him on.

"*Scoot, scoot, scoot that booty-booty!*"

Once again, Cyborg presses the button on his robotic chest. *Click!*
And once again, the bass-kickin' music starts to bump and thump until...

"BOOTY!"

"Well, if he wants to stay, he's gotta do the Booty Scooty," Cyborg tells him.
"ARGH!" Freak groans. "Come on!"

"Sorry, bro," says
Cyborg. "Tower rules."

"Oh yeah! Did you hear that, Freak?" Beast Boy asks his newfound friend.

Raven cringes at the sight of the creature. "You brought him in the house?"

"Yeah," Beast Boy replies. "Likes I said, we both love turnips, so we're best friends."

Just then, Robin has a brilliant idea. "Wait one second!" he says. "Why don't we sell this extremely valuable map? It's worth a fortune!"

"Ugh," Raven grumbles. "That's what we said at the beginning!"

"And you insisted we go on that super-dangerous adventure," adds Cyborg.

Robin ignores them. "We'll sell the map!"

"Then the Tower is saved?" asks Starfire.

Robin nods. "We are going to live in this tower now...and for the rest of our lives!"

The Titans all cheer!